The Small Potatoes Go Camping

by Josh Selig
illustrated by Cassandra Gibbons

Grosset & Dunlap
An Imprint of Penguin Group (USA) Inc.

Copyright © 2013 by Little Airplane Productions, Inc. "SMALL POTATOES" CHARACTERS AND LOGOS © and ™ 2013 LITTLE AIRPLANE PRODUCTIONS, INC. All rights reserved. Published by Grosset & Dunlap, a division of Penguin Young Readers Group, 345 Hudson Street, New York, New York 10014. GROSSET & DUNLAP is a trademark of Penguin Group (USA) Inc. Manufactured in China.

ISBN 978-0-448-46366-7   10 9 8 7 6 5 4 3 2 1

ALWAYS LEARNING

PEARSON

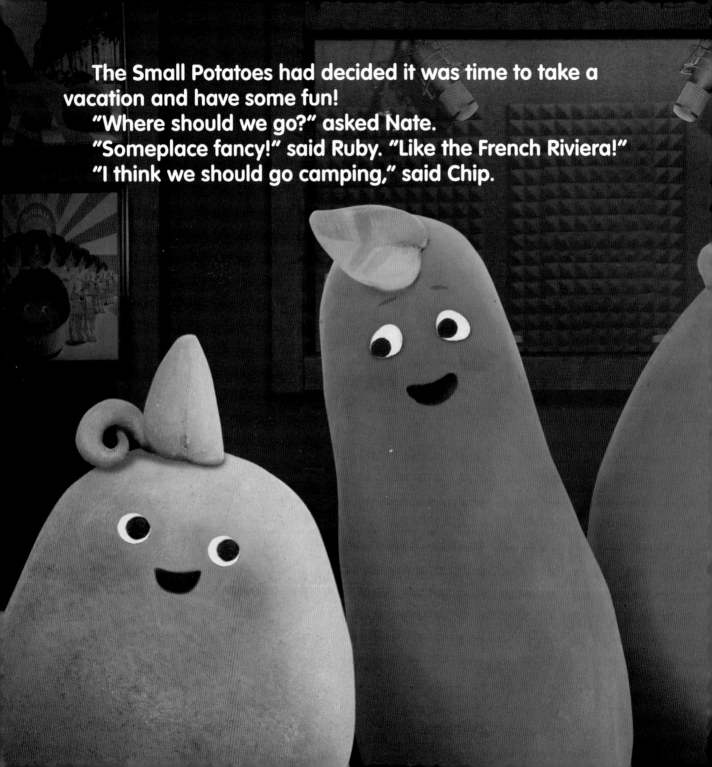

The Small Potatoes had decided it was time to take a vacation and have some fun!

"Where should we go?" asked Nate.

"Someplace fancy!" said Ruby. "Like the French Riviera!"

"I think we should go camping," said Chip.

"Oh, I love to camp!" said Olaf. "Especially toasting marshmallows. Yum!"

Ruby wasn't thrilled about going camping, but she agreed to go, anyway.

"I'll just have to make the best of it," said Ruby.

Nate, Olaf, and Chip packed everything they needed for their camping trip and got ready to hike off into the woods. But Ruby was nowhere to be seen.

"Where's Ruby?" asked Nate.
"She's still packing," said Olaf.
"I think she's bringing a lot of stuff," said Chip.
"Excuse me! Can I get some help, please?" called Ruby.

Nate, Olaf, and Chip rushed over to find Ruby surrounded by lots of pink suitcases.
"What's in all these suitcases, Ruby?" asked Nate.

"They are full of all the things I'm going to need," Ruby said. "All my dresses, all my cute hats, and of course, all my pretty scarves. Just because we're going camping doesn't mean I shouldn't look nice."

"Okay, Ruby," Nate said with a shrug. "Let's get going!"

When they arrived at their campsite, the Small Potatoes got to work pitching their tent. It was a beautiful night for camping.

"Now we need to find some dry wood to make a campfire!" said Nate.

The Small Potatoes gathered up lots of small twigs for the campfire. Just when they were about to light the fire and toast their marshmallows, the sky got very cloudy and dark!

Then it began to rain. It rained very hard. And the wind started blowing. *Whoosh! Whoosh!* All the Small Potatoes ran inside their tent to stay dry.

Inside the tent, the Small Potatoes huddled together.
"This is a very big storm!" said Chip.
"Yeah, I hope our marshmallows don't get wet!" said Olaf.

"Don't worry, everything is going to be okay," said Nate.
"We should have gone to the French Riviera," said Ruby.

Just then a big gust of wind came along and blew their tent away! *Whooooooooshhhhh!* "Uh-oh! There goes the tent!" said Olaf.

"Wow! That was one strong gust of wind!" said Chip.
"It sure was," said Nate, "but it looks like the rain is stopping.
Everything is going to be okay."

Ruby rolled her eyes. "I never did like camping," she said.

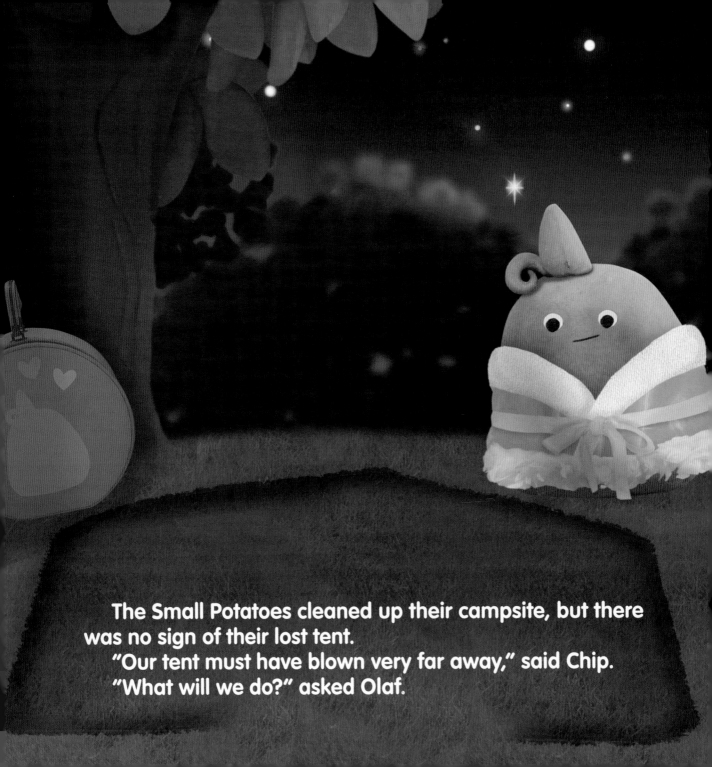

The Small Potatoes cleaned up their campsite, but there was no sign of their lost tent.

"Our tent must have blown very far away," said Chip.

"What will we do?" asked Olaf.

"We'll just have to make something else to sleep under tonight," said Nate. "Let's find some leaves and some branches and see if that will work."

"Leaves and branches?" asked Ruby.

"It's worth a try," said Nate.

The Small Potatoes gathered leaves and branches
and tried to build a shelter for the night.

But it didn't work out so well. The leaves and branches just didn't make a good shelter.

The Small Potatoes didn't know what to do. They had no tent, and it was getting very late. They hadn't made a campfire or toasted even one marshmallow!

"I really would like a marshmallow," said Olaf.

Suddenly Ruby had an idea!
"I know! Maybe we can make a tent out of things in my suitcases!"

"Well, it's certainly worth a try!" said Nate.
The Small Potatoes got to work making a tent out of
all of Ruby's beautiful things. They worked very hard.

The Small Potatoes made the most wonderful tent ever!
Ruby's colorful dresses were tied to her cute hats and pretty
scarves. The Small Potatoes sat outside their tent and roasted
marshmallows on the campfire!

"That was a great idea, Ruby," said Chip.
"Yes, well, I do have my moments," said Ruby.
"You know what? Camping isn't so bad after all!"

What are your favorite things to do on a campout?